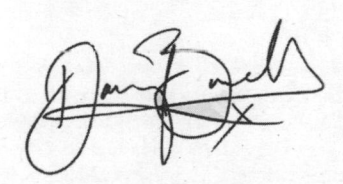

Magic
Ballerina ™

*Rosa a...* wishes

Welcome to the world of ...

I have always loved to dance. The captivating
music and wonderful stories of ballet are so
inspiring. So come with me and let's follow
Rosa on her magical adventures in
Enchantia, where the stories of dance will
take you on a very special journey.

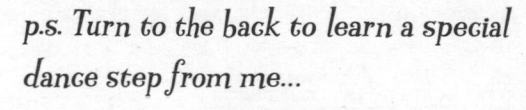

p.s. Turn to the back to learn a special
dance step from me...

Special thanks to
Linda Chapman and
Nellie Ryan

First published in Great Britain by HarperCollins Children's Books 2009
HarperCollins Children's Books is a division of HarperCollins Publishers Ltd,
77-85 Fulham Palace Road, Hammersmith, London W6 8JB

The HarperCollins website address is
www.harpercollins.co.uk

4

Text copyright © HarperCollins Children's Books 2009
Illustrations by Nellie Ryan
Illustrations copyright © HarperCollins Children's Books 2009

MAGIC BALLERINA™ and the 'Magic Ballerina' logo are
trademarks of HarperCollins Publishers Ltd.

ISBN-13 978 0 00 730034 1

Printed and bound in England by
Clays Ltd, St Ives plc

**Mixed Sources**
Product group from well-managed
forests and other controlled sources
www.fsc.org  Cert no. SW-COC-1806
© 1996 Forest Stewardship Council

FSC is a non-profit international organisation established to promote the
responsible management of the world's forests. Products carrying the FSC
label are independently certified to assure consumers that they come
from forests that are managed to meet the social, economic and
ecological needs of present and future generations.

Find out more about HarperCollins and the environment at
www.harpercollins.co.uk/green

# Magic Ballerina™

## Rosa and the Three Wishes

# Darcey Bussell

HarperCollins *Children's Books*

*To Phoebe and Zoe, as they are the inspiration behind Magic Ballerina.*

# Contents

# Prologue

*In the soft, pale light, the girl stood
with her head bent and her hands
held lightly in front of her.
There was a moment's silence and then the
first notes of the music began.
For as long as the girl could remember
music had seemed to tell her of
another world – a magical, exciting
world – that lay far, far away.
She always felt if she could just
close her eyes and lose herself,
then she would get there.
Maybe this time. As the music
swirled inside her, she swept
her arms above her head, rose on to
her toes and began to dance…*

# The Last Day

"Isn't it weird to think that it's our very last day here?" Rosa said as she and her best friend, Olivia, walked into the changing rooms at Madame Za-Za's ballet school.

Olivia nodded in agreement. After the holidays they would both be going to the Royal Ballet School in London!

Rosa looked round at the familiar green

walls and rows of pegs for hanging their
clothes on and breathed in the smell of
hairspray. "I'm really going to miss this
place," she sighed, taking off her coat.

"Me too," agreed Olivia.

Rosa thought of everything Madame Za-Za
had taught her since she had started at the
school – and everything that had happened
to her, not just the classes, and the exams
and the performances…

Taking her red ballet
shoes out of her bag, she
smiled to herself. She had
a secret. Her shoes were
magic! Sometimes they
would start to glisten and
glow and then they would

whisk her away to Enchantia, a land where all the characters from the different ballets lived. Rosa had been on some fantastic magical adventures there.

*But the shoes will still take me to Enchantia even when I'm at the Royal Ballet School,* she thought, stroking the soft leather. *I don't have to say goodbye to them.*

She felt slightly uneasy though. She hated to admit it, but it almost seemed as if the shoes belonged here, with her ballet teacher, Madame Za-Za. It had been Madame Za-Za who had given them to Delphie Durand, and then Delphie had passed them on to Rosa.

Trying not to think about it, Rosa got changed. She was just tying the ribbons on her shoes when a girl walked into the

changing rooms, her chin held high. She had bright green eyes and brown hair.

Rosa groaned inwardly. *Holly!*

Holly was a new pupil at Madame Za-Za's ballet school. She had recently come to live in the town with her aunt and uncle, and had started in Rosa and Olivia's class. She was very good at ballet but she knew it and, although she was a little younger than most of the other girls, she seemed put out that she wasn't in the highest class.

"I want to sit there," she said to Rosa. She pointed at the bench where Rosa's bag was and gave an imperious toss of her head. "Move your bag."

Rosa frowned. "No. There are plenty of other places you can sit."

"But I want to get changed there because it is next to the radiator," Holly told her.

Taking off her coat she threw it down, covering up Rosa's clothes, and then she went into the little sideroom where the sinks and toilets were.

Rosa's temper flared. She jumped to her

feet and grabbed Holly's coat, intending to dump it on the floor.

"Don't," Olivia said quickly. "It's our last day."

"But you saw what she just did!" Rosa exclaimed.

"But after today we won't ever have to see her again," Olivia pointed out. "Don't have a row, Rosa. Please." Some of the other girls had started to come in and were looking at Rosa and Olivia curiously.

Rosa forced herself to calm down. Olivia was right. It was their last lesson; she didn't want to ruin it.

"Just ignore her and let's go and warm up," said Olivia. "'I want to make the most of every second today."

"Me too," Rosa agreed and put the coat down. They smiled and hurried out of the changing rooms.

It was hard to ignore Holly. She argued with Madame Za-Za when the teacher corrected her movements in the exercises. She tutted at the other girls when they got in her way. Rosa felt cross. She found it hard to enjoy her last class when Holly was being so awful all of the time.

"I want you to imagine you are a butterfly emerging

17

from a chrysalis," Madame Za-Za said as they sat and listened to a piece of beautiful music. "You are stretching your wings, the colours sparkling and glowing, and then with a burst of energy you start to fly, swirling and swooping…"

As Madame Za-Za's voice and the music swept over them, Rosa longed to get up and start dancing.

"And now the butterfly's energy is fading. Its life is coming to an end," Madame Za-Za said as the music slowed. "It pauses, flies on, pauses, flies on, until finally it lands for the very last time."

It was time to dance. The girls ran to find a space in the studio. The music swelled out again and Rosa imagined

herself as the butterfly pushing out of a chrysalis. It was wonderful to swirl and spin, imagining she was as light as air, soaring through the sky and then gradually slowing down and coming to rest.

Madame Za-Za split them into two groups so they could watch each other.

"Look at Holly," Olivia whispered as she and Rosa sat on the floor. Holly was

moving lightly, her body expressing joy
and flight. But it was as the music started
to slow that Rosa found she couldn't take
her eyes off her.  With every pause, the
dark-haired girl seemed to get a little weaker.
Her arms, lifted behind her like wings,
seemed to be gradually losing their
strength, fingers fluttering.
Every movement she made
expressed sadness, the
coming to a life's end.
As the music finished,
she took three last steps
forward and then sank
to her knees, her arms
folding around her,
head sinking down.

"Oh, wow!" Rosa breathed, despite her dislike. "She's brilliant."

"Amazing," agreed Olivia.

"Excellent girls," Madame Za-Za said at the end of the lesson. "There has been some really good work today. We'll finish there." She curtseyed and they all curtseyed back.

As Rosa and Olivia collected their character skirts from the end of the room, Rosa saw Holly walking nearby, her face composed.

"Your free dancing was brilliant," Rosa said generously.

Holly shrugged as if to say *of course* and walked away.

"Honestly!" Rosa exclaimed crossly to Olivia. "She is so rude!"

"Rosa!" It was Madame Za-Za.

Rosa looked round.

"Would you mind coming to my office for a quick word?" the teacher asked with a smile.

# The Ballet Shoes

"Sit down, Rosa," Madame Za-Za said, patting the sofa. Rosa sat. She loved Madame Za-Za's office. The walls were covered with ballet photographs and there were shelves of books and a large desk, as well as the sofa.

"So, it was your last lesson today," Madame Za-Za said. "I will miss you very

much. I hope you will come back and visit
when you are home in the holidays."

"Oh yes, I'll come lots," Rosa said eagerly.
She only lived just around the corner.

Madame Za-Za steepled
her fingers. "Before you go,
I want to talk to you about
the ballet shoes."

Rosa felt herself stiffen
slightly. Was Madame
Za-Za going to ask for
them back?

Her ballet teacher
seemed to read her mind. "I know they
belong to you, but soon the time will come
when you should pass the shoes on. They
are only ever really lent to us, Rosa. And

whilst the person who wears them helps the people in the land of Enchantia, the magic of the shoes is such that they also help the wearer too." Her eyes gazed into Rosa's. "There may be someone around you, Rosa, who needs that help."

Rosa frowned. Everyone in her dance class seemed happy enough, everyone apart from…

She stared at her ballet teacher. "Not Holly!"

Madame Za-Za held her eyes with a steady gaze.

"But, Madame Za-Za, she doesn't need help, she's rude and…" Rosa broke off, suddenly realising her voice was getting louder and louder.

Madame Za-za spoke softly, "Sometimes everything is not quite as it seems. I told Delphie that once."

Rosa's mind guiltily flashed back to how she had acted when she had first been given the shoes. She'd been defensive and prickly and hadn't made friends easily. Not only that, but she'd rushed into things too quickly and lost her temper too fast. Her adventures in Enchantia had taught her a lot. But, even so...

"Not Holly," she said in a low voice, shaking her head. "Please don't tell me I have to give them to her."

"I am not going to tell you to give them to anyone," Madame Za-Za reassured her. "That decision is yours. But do not judge

Holly only by what you see. She has not had an easy life." She patted Rosa's hand. "Your heart will tell you what to do, my dear. Go now. I'm very proud of you – both as a dancer and as a person." She stood up and as Rosa stood up too, the teacher kissed her lightly on both cheeks. "Good luck, Rosa."

"Thank you," Rosa said softly. She walked slowly to the changing rooms, her

mind turning over everything Madame
Za-Za had said.

An image of Holly dancing the end
of the butterfly dance filled Rosa's mind.
She saw again the intense sadness in the
younger girl's face and Madame Za-Za's
words echoed back to her: *Holly has not had
an easy life.*

Rosa felt torn. She respected Madame
Za-Za so hugely, it felt wrong to go against
what the teacher had been saying. But she
couldn't bear the thought of letting Holly
have her precious shoes.

*She probably wouldn't want them anyway,*
Rosa told herself as she walked into the
changing rooms. *I bet she'd just turn her nose
up and say they weren't good enough for someone*

*who was as brilliant a dancer*
*as she was and…*

Rosa stopped dead.
The rooms were empty
now apart from Holly.
She was sitting on the
bench reading a letter.
Hearing Rosa come in she
looked up. Rosa saw the
tracks of tears on her cheeks.

Jumping to her feet and looking
embarrassed, Holly quickly thrust the
letter in her bag.

"Are you OK?" Rosa asked.

"I'm fine!"

But Rosa could hear the tears in the other
girl's voice. She went over to her. "Holly…"

"Leave me alone. I said I'm fine!" Holly pushed past her and hurried out of the changing rooms. Rosa looked at the bench and realised Holly had left her coat behind. She started to go to the door and call her back but just then she felt her feet start to tingle.

She glanced down. Her red shoes were sparkling and glowing!

"Oh, wow!" she gasped, her heart leaping. She was off to Enchantia again!

# An Angry Crowd

Rosa felt herself spinning through the air in a cloud of bright colours. After a few moments, she was set down lightly. She looked around and saw that she was standing on a cobbled street in a quaint town. The houses were tall and thin, and the shops were old-fashioned with curving front windows.

A crowd of people were gathered at one
end of the street outside a large, double-
fronted shop with a sign that said *Leonardo's
Toy and Model Shop*. The crowd seemed to be
calling out to someone who was standing
on the steps in front of the door.

"Let us in!"

"We need to buy presents!"

"My son's birthday is tomorrow and
I must buy him a toy!"

*What's going on?* thought Rosa curiously.
She made her way to the back of the crowd.

"You have to let us in!" several people
cried together.

"I'm really, really sorry, but I can't," the
person on the steps said desperately. "The
shop's closed."

*Nutmeg!* thought Rosa, immediately
recognising the voice of her friend, the Fairy
of the Spices. Rosa wriggled her way through
the gaps to the front of the crowd and saw the
fairy in her pink and pale brown tutu
standing on the steps that led to the shop.
Her silvery wings were fluttering slightly and
she was looking upset, dancing on her toes in
agitation. "Please go away," she begged,
looking at the people.

The crowd around
Rosa started muttering
angrily. Rosa slipped
to one side. "Nutmeg!"
she called.

Nutmeg's face lit up.
"Rosa!"

"What's going
on?" Rosa demanded
as the fairy ran lightly down the steps.

"Oh, it's awful!" Nutmeg's brown eyes
looked anxious. "Leonardo, the toymaker,
has shut his shop and everyone is getting
really cross." Nutmeg glanced around at the
crowd who were starting to push and shove
each other now. "I've got to do something.
There's going to be a riot soon. They all want

34

to get into the shop but he won't open it!"

"Can't you distract them?" Rosa suggested. "Why don't you magic up some food or something?"

"Great idea!" gasped Nutmeg. "Oh, Rosa, I'm so glad you're here!"

She pulled a magic wand out of a pocket in her tutu and waved it. There was a silver flash and suddenly there in the street was a big table laid out with currant buns and hot chocolate sprinkled with nutmeg!

The crowd looked around, their angry mutterings fading as the delicious scents floated towards them.

"Help yourselves!" Nutmeg called. "Please, everyone. While you eat, I'll try to persuade Leonardo to open his shop."

Looking surprised and pleased, the people turned from the steps and crowded around the table instead. Nutmeg's shoulders sagged. "Phew! Oh, Rosa. We've got such a problem here. I hope you can help."

"I'll try," Rosa said. The shoes always brought her to Enchantia whenever the people there needed her help. "What's been happening?"

"I'll tell you inside." Nutmeg looked at

the crowd. "But maybe we'd better use the back door!"

Nutmeg led the way in through the back of the shop. Rosa gasped. There were amazing toys everywhere! There was a fairy doll dancing on a shelf, a rocking horse who was snorting and nodding his head, a row of teddy bears who looked so real you could almost imagine them hugging you and shelf after shelf of models with handles and buttons, many of them moving and making noises. A toy monkey was working an organ on one side of the room. Sweet notes flooded out and all over the ceiling were twinkling fairy lights. It was like being in an enchanted cave!

"Leonardo is the best toymaker in
Enchantia," Nutmeg explained. "Everyone
loves his toys and models. Even grown-ups.
He puts a little bit of toy magic into each

and every one of them, to make them special. He's through here." She led the way towards a door. As she pushed it open, Rosa saw a man in a cloak sitting at a desk, his head in his hands.

"Leonardo, this is Rosa," said Nutmeg. "She's going to try and help."

The man looked around. He had a pointed black beard and black hair, the wrinkles on his face were kind but his eyes looked very sad. "Please help," he begged her. "Please get my Coppelia back."

Rosa looked uncertainly at Nutmeg.

"Leonardo made a doll called Coppelia…" the fairy began to explain.

"The most beautiful doll you ever saw," broke in Leonardo. "She looked just like a

real person. When you
wound her up she
would walk and talk.
She was like a
child to me and
kept me
company as she
danced and
moved around
the shop, but now
she's gone and
without her
I don't want to
make toys any more!"

"Now everyone's getting really cross because
they can't buy presents," added Nutmeg.

"So where is Coppelia?" Rosa asked.

Nutmeg took a deep breath. "She's been stolen by King Rat!"

"King Rat!" Rosa echoed. King Rat was one of the few horrible characters in Enchantia. He lived in a smelly castle with his fierce mouse guards and hated dancing. "But why would he steal her?"

"He wants to get married," explained Nutmeg. "Princess Aurelia refused to marry him a while ago so he's been looking for someone else. He decided Coppelia would be the perfect bride."

"But she's just a doll," said Rosa, confused.

Leonardo sighed. "Yes, but when King Rat stole her, he also stole a crystal orb I had made recently. It has the power to give three wishes to any person who throws it

into the air. I, as its maker, cannot use
those wishes, but King Rat can and he is
planning to use it to
wish Coppelia
alive. He doesn't
know how to
use the orb at
the moment, but
I fear it will not
take him long to
figure it out."

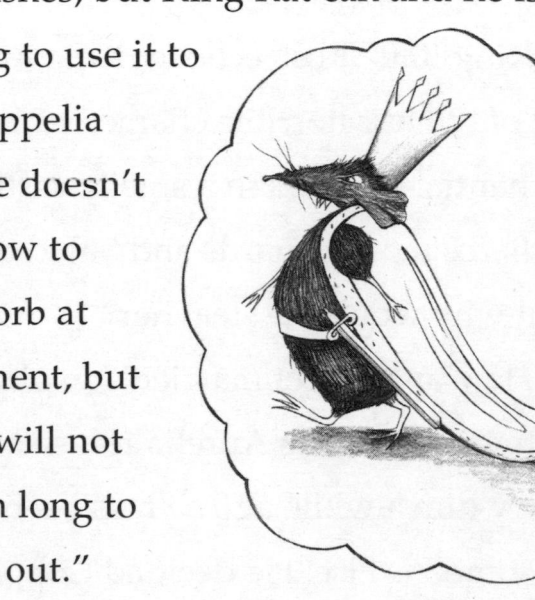

An image of
King Rat flashed
into Rosa's mind –
black greasy fur, pointed teeth, a sharp
sword hanging at his belt and beady red
eyes. She shivered, but forced her chin up.

"We'll just have to go to his castle and get her back!" she said. "Come on, Nutmeg! Let's go!"

# 4

# King Rat's Castle

"See you later, Leonardo!" Nutmeg called.

"I hope so!" replied the toymaker.

She waved her wand. Pink and silver
sparkles surrounded her and Rosa, and
they were swept away by the magic. A few
moments later they were set down in the
woods outside King Rat's castle. King Rat
had cast spells to make sure that no one else

could work any powerful magic in his castle and its grounds, so Nutmeg's magic couldn't take them closer than the edge of the woods.

Rosa peered through the trees at the black foreboding castle. There was an expanse of muddy grass covered with puddles between them and the castle door.

Nutmeg looked anxious. "How are we going to get in?"

Rosa didn't know. They'd tried to sneak into King Rat's castle in the past and it had never been easy. "There are some windows open." She pointed at a couple of the ground-floor windows that were ajar. "We could climb through those."

"But what if we're seen?"

Rosa saw the fear on the fairy's face.

"Don't worry. I can always go in on my own. You stay here."

"No way!" Nutmeg protested. "I'm coming with you."

They ran across the muddy grass towards the castle. Rosa's heart beat fast. Where was King Rat? Was he in the castle? They reached the large windows. Through them, Rosa could see the Great Hall with a stool at the end. Sitting on it was a life-sized doll with pale blonde hair in plaits, a bonnet and big blue eyes. She looked so real, Rosa almost expected her to move!

"Coppelia!" breathed Nutmeg. "That's her, Rosa! And look!" She pointed to a table near the doll. On it was a sparkling glass ball. "That's the magic orb!"

Rosa's mind raced. "OK," she whispered. "Let's get into the hall, grab Coppelia and the orb and run back to the woods. Then you can magic us away, Nutmeg." Her breath was short in her throat, her palms damp. There was no one around. This could be their chance!

"Come on!" She started to climb through the window.

They landed inside as quietly as they could, but just as they had started to run towards Coppelia, there was the sound of heavy boots on a staircase. Nutmeg grabbed Rosa's arm and pulled her into a curtained alcove. As the curtain swished closed behind them, Rosa heard the sound of voices.

"Can we have lunch now, Sire?" an eager

voice said. "Cook's made chicken pie."

Rosa tweaked the edge of the curtain

back. King Rat was
standing by the table,
wearing a black cloak
with a white fur trim
around it.

"Oh, very well!" he
snapped to the two mouse
guards. "But before you
go, how do I look in my
finery?" King Rat patted
his cloak.

"Like a girl…" one of the
mice started to say before
the one standing beside
him kicked him sharply.

"You look really… really majestic, your majesty!" he told the king.

King Rat ran a paw vainly through his whiskers. "I do, don't I?" He picked up the orb. "When I manage to make this rotten thing work and my future bride beholds me, she will be swept away by my good looks. What will she be?"

He looked expectantly at his guards.

"Swept away by your good looks," said the second mouse quickly.

He kicked the first one again.

"Yes, yes, quite swept away, Sire," the first mouse echoed.

King Rat looked pleased. "Good. You may go!"

The mice scampered off gratefully. King Rat strode over to the doll, his red eyes gleaming. "I wish for Coppelia to come to life!" he declared, shaking the orb.

But nothing happened.

"He's got to throw it, hasn't he?" whispered Rosa, remembering what the toymaker had said.

Nutmeg nodded.

King Rat swept the ball through the air in a complicated pattern. "I wish for Coppelia to come to life!"

Still nothing happened.

King Rat tried rubbing the orb. "Come on, come on, you stupid useless thing! Work, will you?

52

I wish for Coppelia to come to life."

When nothing happened that time either, he stamped his foot. "Ga!" He thrust the orb in his pocket. "I'll try again after lunch!" And with that, he strode away.

Rosa turned to Nutmeg. "But why doesn't he just use his own magic to bring her to life?"

"King Rat's very powerful, but only toy magic from the toymaker is able to do something like that," said Nutmeg. "The orb is full of it."

Rosa looked back at the doll. She was worried it wasn't going to take King Rat long to figure out how to make the orb give him the wishes. "We need to get Coppelia out of here and then somehow get the orb away from King Rat. We could take

Coppelia now while everyone's at lunch and get out there," she said, pointing to a small window in the wall behind them.

"But then King Rat will come back and find she's gone," Nutmeg said.

Rosa frowned. "Hmm."

"Oh, it's useless!" muttered Nutmeg.

"No it's not!" Rosa said, a plan coming into her mind. "Why don't I swap places with Coppelia? You can sneak her out of here to the woods and then I'll see if I can find a way to get the orb off King Rat. I could even pretend to come to life so he thinks the orb has worked! Then he might put

it down or something and I can grab it."

"But what if King Rat realises it's you pretending to be the doll?" protested Nutmeg.

"I'll just have to make sure he doesn't," Rosa replied. "I won't have to fool him for long. Once I've made him think he's brought me to life, I'll ask him to go and fetch me something. Then while he's away, I'll take the orb and you, me and Coppelia can all escape."

Nutmeg still looked unsure.

Rosa ducked out through the curtains. "Trust me. It'll work!" she said. "I know it will!"

# Tricking King Rat!

Ten minutes later, Coppelia was in the alcove dressed in Rosa's ballet clothes and Rosa was sitting on the stool wearing the doll's red and white dress. Luckily, her hair was the same colour as the doll's. Rosa had tied it up in plaits and pulled the bonnet down over her face.

"You look perfect!" Nutmeg told her.

Just then there was the sound of a door slamming. Nutmeg raced back to the alcove as King Rat strode into the hall with the orb in his hand. "Time to try again!" he declared, wiping chicken pie off his whiskers with the back of one paw. "Now, let's see what haven't I tried…?"

*Please don't throw it*, Rosa prayed. To her relief, King Rat didn't. Instead, he breathed on it. "I wish Coppelia would come to life!"

Rosa put her head up sharply.

"W… what?" King Rat stared at her. "It must have worked!"

Rosa heard the sound of music swelling out. It was Nutmeg! Even though the fairy couldn't do strong magic in the castle, she could still manage to do a little bit, and

making music play was one of the easiest
magical things to do in Enchantia.

Rosa had watched the ballet of *Coppelia*,
where the ballerina acted as if she was a
doll coming to life. She moved her hands
sharply down to her sides, keeping every
movement precise. The music really helped.
She drummed her toes quickly on the floor,
perfectly in time with the short, quick beats
of the music and then stood up.

King Rat stared as if he couldn't believe
his eyes. The music swelled into a waltz and
Rosa set off round the room, turning and
spinning, moving at first like a mechanical
doll, but then trying to make her movements
smoother so that it seemed as if she was
turning into a real person. She stopped in fifth
position and looked at the floor as the music
faded. Her heart was beating faster than
ever. Had she fooled King Rat?

"My love! My sweet! You've come to life!"
King Rat exclaimed.

*Yes!* Rosa thought.

He walked around her, looking her up and
down. "You don't look quite so beautiful now
though," he said frowning. "You're scrawnier,
your cheeks look paler…"

Rosa quickly covered her face with her hand as if she was shy. "But I am Coppelia!" she said, making her voice as light and musical as she could. Her heart felt as if it was in her throat.

To her relief, King Rat shrugged. "Oh, well, you'll do. We shall be married this very evening, my love, and you will live here with me forever."

"Oh, good!" Rosa enthused, trying to sound as if she meant it.

He put the orb down on the table. Rosa looked at it. If she could just get to it…

King Rat strode to her and twisted his mouth into what he obviously thought was a charming smile. "I am sure you are thinking how lucky you are to have a rat

like me for your future husband. Would you like to kiss me, my dear?"

To Rosa's horror, he shut his eyes and pursed his pie-smeared whiskery lips for a kiss.

"Um!" she stepped backwards quickly. "Not until… until I have an engagement ring, my… um… my love." The thought of kissing King Rat was just too horrible!

King Rat frowned but didn't argue. "Oh, very well. I will call for my carriage and go and choose one." He started to stride across the hall.

Rosa's heart leaped; maybe this was going to be her chance to get the orb!

But just then, King Rat's eyes fell on it and he gave a sudden laugh. "But of course, I don't need to go anywhere. I can wish for a ring! I've got two wishes left, after all."

Rosa almost squeaked in fright. If King Rat made a wish and it didn't work, he'd realise he'd been tricked. How could she stop him? But it was too late. King Rat had already picked up the orb!

# Wishing Magic

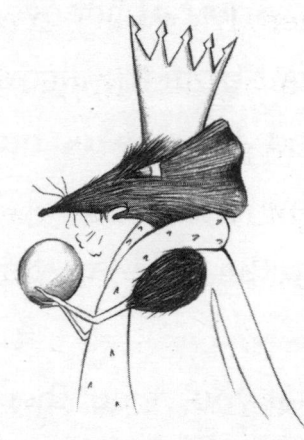

"I wish for an engagement ring!" King Rat declared, breathing on the orb.

Rosa's heart pounded. When nothing happened, King Rat looked confused, and then cross. A frown deepened on his face. "I wish for an engagement ring!" he repeated, more loudly and angrily.

Suddenly, there was a faint tinkle of

music. "Ah, maybe it's working!" said
King Rat.

Out of the corner of her eye, Rosa saw a
note flutter out from the alcove. King Rat
hadn't noticed. He was too busy looking
round. "But where's the ring?"

Rosa ran to the note. As she read it, her
heart lifted.

"What's that you've got there, my love?"
King Rat said.

"It's a note for you," Rosa said innocently,
turning round.

King Rat took the paper. "*Look in the woods
for the ring you want to find. Magic has placed
it there so your hearts may be entwined.*" He
blinked. "The ring's in the woods!" he
exclaimed in astonishment.

"I suppose you didn't actually say you
wanted the ring *here*," Rosa pointed out.
She was sure she knew what was happening.
If Nutmeg could get them to the woods she
could use her own magic to conjure up a ring
herself.

"Useless orb! Now I've got to go
outside," King Rat grumbled.

Rosa glanced out of the window and saw
Nutmeg racing across the grass towards the

trees. King Rat couldn't go out now! She ran
over and stopped in front of him. "Dance
with me before you go," she said quickly.

"I hate dancing!" King Rat frowned.

"So it would prove how much you loved
me if you did dance with me," said Rosa.
"Just once round the room."
She grabbed hold of King
Rat in a waltzing
position. "Here
we go!"

"But… but…"
King Rat
spluttered.
"NO!"

"One, two,
three. One, two

three," Rosa waltzed a struggling King Rat
around the room until saw Nutmeg reach
the trees and then she caught sight of a faint
silver flash. Hopefully that meant Nutmeg
had worked her magic! With a sigh of
relief, Rosa let King Rat go. "You
*do* love me!" She fluttered her eyelashes
at him. "Now can we go and see if my
engagement ring is there, my love?"

"You're very demanding," scowled King
Rat. "Dancing one minute, finding you a
ring the next. Huh! I hope you're not going
to be like this when we're married." He
straightened his cloak and then strode out
of the door, putting the orb in his pocket
as he went.

Rosa hurried after him, jumping over the

puddles. As he reached the first tree in the woods, he began hunting around.

"Aha!" He seized something sparkling. "Here it is!" he said, straightening up with a ring. "Now, I shall propose to you."

"Wonderful!" Rosa gasped. "But you must get changed before you ask me to marry you. You're dreadfully dirty."

King Rat looked down at his mud-spattered clothes. "That's the very last thing I'm doing!"

"I won't ask for

anything else," promised Rosa, hoping she was right.

As King Rat strode away, she saw Nutmeg peep out from behind a tree and they gave each other a quick thumbs up. Rosa hastened after King Rat.

Back in the hall, he threw off his cloak. "Wait here, Coppelia," he commanded. "I will return as soon as I have changed my clothes."

He stomped away up the stairs. Rosa didn't waste a second. She grabbed the orb from the pocket of his cloak and ran to the alcove. Nutmeg was just climbing back in through the window.

"I've got the orb!" Rosa gasped.

"Brilliant!" Nutmeg looked at the glittering

ball. "There's so much magic inside it, Rosa. It really shouldn't be in the hands of someone like King Rat. Let's get Coppelia to the woods while King Rat is changing and I'll use my magic to whisk us away. We mustn't use the orb's amazing magic for something I can do easily. It's too precious."

They started pulling the doll towards the window but she was stiff and hard to manoeuvre.

"Oh, I wish she really was alive!" Rosa said in frustration. As the words left her lips she lost her grip on the orb. She caught it instinctively. There was a tinkling sound like an old-fashioned music box playing and suddenly Coppelia blinked and smiled!

Rosa and Nutmeg both gasped.

"I… I didn't mean to make a wish!" Rosa exclaimed.

Coppelia stretched her arms above her head. "Hello."

Rosa and Nutmeg exchanged horrified looks.

Coppelia turned on her toes and stopped in fifth position. "I'm alive!" she cried.

"Sssh!" Nutmeg hushed her quickly.

"This wasn't part of the plan," said Rosa staring at the doll.

"Look, let's just get her to the woods and

get out of here," said
Nutmeg climbing out of
the window. "Coppelia,
come with us."

Coppelia looked at
her in surprise. "Is
walking through
windows what you do
when you are alive?"

"Oh, yes," Nutmeg
told her.

"If you want to
escape from King Rat
that is," Rosa muttered.
The three of them
climbed through the
window and jumped

down. Rosa grabbed the doll's hand but as she did so, Rosa heard King Rat's voice from inside the hall. "Coppelia! Where are you, my love?"

"Here I am!" cried Coppelia merrily.

"No!" Rosa cried in horror. "Coppelia, shush!"

"You're outside?" King Rat said in astonishment.

"Yes!" cried Coppelia as Rosa started trying to pull her towards the woods.

The large front door flew open and King Rat came charging out in his cream and gold wedding clothes. He was so astonished when he saw Rosa, Nutmeg and Coppelia that he skidded to a halt. "What? How? Who?" he spluttered, pointing.

His boots slipped on the muddy ground and the next moment he had tumbled over into a puddle. He sat up, mud and water dripping from his ears and whiskers. "It's all a trick! Guards! Get them!" he roared.

"Time for a wish!" gasped Rosa.

"Yes! Use the orb, Rosa! This is an emergency!" said Nutmeg.

Grabbing the orb from her pocket, Rosa threw it into the air. "I wish that me, Nutmeg and Coppelia were all back in the toyshop, RIGHT NOW!"

The guards came running to the door but they were too late. There was a flash of pink light and Rosa and the others were suddenly whisked away!

# The Final Wish

Rosa, Nutmeg and Coppelia landed in a heap on the floor of the toyshop. Leonardo, who was still sitting at his desk, jumped to his feet. "What's going on? His eyes fell on the doll. "Coppelia!"

"Father!" Coppelia cried.

Leonardo went so pale, Rosa thought he was going to faint. "You can talk!"

Rosa scrambled to her feet. She wasn't sure how to explain. "Um, we've got Coppelia back but well, as you can see we... we accidentally managed to bring her to life."

"We could use the orb's last wish to turn her back," said Nutmeg quickly.

The toymaker ignored her. He strode over to Coppelia and gently helped her up. "Coppelia, my child." He touched her face as if he didn't dare to believe it. "You're alive. I always

wanted you to be, but I couldn't use the magic in the orb I had made for my own good. Someone else had to wish for it, wanting it for themselves. This is like a dream come true."

Coppelia hugged him. "But it's not a dream, it's real. Now, I can help you run the shop, Father. Oh, it'll be wonderful." She spun round on the spot. "I'll be able to help people choose presents, and run the till and you'll have more time to make toys and models." She stopped in front of him and took his hands. "I'm so happy, Father!"

"And so am I." Leonardo turned to the girls and they saw the tears of delight in his eyes. "This is the best day of my life!" he declared. "What happened?"

Nutmeg quickly told him everything while Coppelia and Rosa swapped clothes again.

"It was so funny when that silly King Rat ended up in the puddle!" giggled Coppelia. "I'm very glad I don't have to marry him!"

"I'm really sorry we used up two of the wishes," Rosa said to the toymaker apologetically.

"We weren't going to use the second wish but we had to, or we wouldn't have escaped," put in Nutmeg.

"You did the right thing," Leonardo told

them. "It's far more important that you all got back safely."

"There's still one wish left," Nutmeg pointed out.

Rosa handed the orb to Leonardo. "Here it is."

But the toymaker handed it back. "You have the wish. Both of you. I should never have made the orb. It's too dangerous an object to have lying around. King Rat could try and steal it again, and wish Coppelia away."

Rosa took the orb. A wish! Wow! "What should we wish for?" she asked Nutmeg.

"I don't know," said Nutmeg. "I can do magic myself so I don't need to wish for things like new dresses or shoes and I'm

really happy. Maybe we could wish for something for you."

Rosa thought about it. It seemed wrong to waste something as powerful as a wish on a new dress or a toy. And, like Nutmeg, she was really happy. After all, she was about to go to the Royal Ballet School with Olivia. She looked down at her red shoes and suddenly a picture of Holly crying in the changing rooms came into her head and Madame Za-Za's words echoed through her mind: *the time will soon come when you should pass the shoes on. They are only ever really lent to us, Rosa. And whilst the person who wears them helps the people in the land of Enchantia, the magic of the shoes is that they also help the wearer too.*

"I know what I want to wish for," Rosa

said to Nutmeg.

"Go ahead then," said her friend.

Rosa threw the orb into the air. "I wish that I come back to Enchantia again one day and see my friends here, especially Nutmeg." There was a flash of pink light as she caught the glittering ball.

Nutmeg stared. "But Rosa! Why wish that? The shoes will bring you back anyway."

Rosa shook her head. "No, they won't." She swallowed. "It's time I gave them to someone else, Nutmeg. I know it is."

Nutmeg looked dismayed. "But I'll really miss you."

"I'll miss you too," said Rosa.

The toymaker spoke softly. "Don't be sad, either of you. Rosa's wish will be granted."

Relief rushed through Rosa. She knew that if she was sure she would come back one day, then giving the shoes away wouldn't be quite so hard.

"Phew!" said Nutmeg. "I couldn't bear not seeing you again."

"Me neither," said Rosa, hugging her.

The toymaker smiled at them both. "Now I think we should make it up to all those people who have been shut out of the shop. Nutmeg, can you magic up a feast for us?"

"Of course, but why?" asked Nutmeg.

The toymaker threw open his arms. "I want to have a party!"

Five minutes later, the doors of the shop were open and the people from the town were pouring in. The toy monkey was playing a lively tune on the organ and there was a massive table loaded with iced cakes and biscuits in the shapes of all different toys, small sandwiches and bowls overflowing with grapes and chocolate-covered strawberries.

Coppelia was handing out cups of fruit punch and her father was watching proudly. People started to waltz around the room in pairs, dipping and swaying.

Rosa felt the music catching hold of her feet. "Come on!" She grabbed Nutmeg's hands.

They began to waltz, turning as they moved lightly across the floor. *One, two, three. One, two, three…* Rosa counted in her head as they twirled round joyfully. Suddenly, she felt her feet start to tingle. Her ballet shoes were glowing!

"I'm going home!" she cried.

Nutmeg hugged her. "I hope see you again soon, Rosa."

"You will! The magic is going to bring me back one day," said Rosa. "Bye, Nutmeg!" Colours started to swirl around her in a rainbow haze. "See you soon!" she gasped as she was whisked away…

# Holly's New Beginning

Rosa was set down in the changing rooms. Seeing Holly's coat, everything came flooding back. Knowing no time would have passed in the normal world while she'd been gone, she ran to the door. "Holly!"

The other girl was at the end of the hall, just going out of the front door. Rosa could still see the tears on her face.

"You left your coat," said Rosa.

For a moment she thought Holly was just going to walk out anyway, but the girl turned and marched back to the changing rooms. She grabbed her coat from the bench. Rosa darted in front of the door. "Holly. Please don't leave yet. I want to give you something."

The younger girl looked at her suspiciously. "What?"

"My ballet shoes."

Holly looked astonished. "Your shoes!" she said glancing at Rosa's feet.

"Yes." Rosa knelt down and started untying the ribbons with trembling fingers. This was hard, but she was sure she was doing the right thing. "They belonged to my friend, Delphie, and before that to

Madame Za-Za, and I want you to have them now. They're old but they're…" she hesitated, "… very special. She pushed them into Holly's hands, watching closely. When she'd touched the ballet shoes for the first time, she'd felt something happen. It was hard to describe. It was as if the moment she had held them they had started to belong to her and she had wanted to put them on.

She saw Holly's fingers tighten on the shoes and her eyes widen just slightly. Rosa felt as though a tightly coiled spring inside her had suddenly released. She wasn't making a mistake. Holly was the right person to own the shoes now. She was sure of it.

"Why are you giving them to me?" Holly asked, looking up, her eyes perplexed.

"Oh, I need new shoes," Rosa said lightly. "And well, I thought you might like them." She hesitated. "You seem upset about something."

A muscle clenched in Holly's jaw but then she looked at the shoes and it was as if they were working their magic already. Her shoulders seemed to relax. "It's my parents," she said, speaking more quietly than she had ever spoken before to Rosa. "They're divorced. They're both ballet dancers. All my life I've lived with one or other of them, travelling around. It's been difficult, but better than this – being here in this country, having no friends, seeing neither of them, staying with family I hardly

know." Her eyes glistened with tears. "I miss them both so very much."

Rosa began to understand what Madame Za-Za had meant about things often being different under the surface.

"This is the first nice thing anyone has done for me since I got here," Holly said, looking at the shoes.

"It won't be the last nice thing anyone does for you, Holly," Rosa told her softly. "Everyone here is lovely – Madame Za-Za, all the girls in class. You just need to give them a chance." She squeezed the other girl's hands around the shoes. "Enjoy the shoes." She remembered the words Delphie had spoken to her. "I hope you find out just how special they are."

She ran out of the changing rooms.

As she reached the front door of Madame Za-Za's and went through it for the last time she thought about everything that was ahead of her – boarding at the Royal Ballet School, hopefully becoming a real ballerina one day. A whole new world was opening up for her.

She paused on the top step of the dance school, thinking of Nutmeg, and all her friends in Enchantia. *They'll be there waiting for me*, she thought. *Even if I haven't got the red shoes.* Remembering her wish, she smiled happily, shut the door and hurried away.

MADAME ZARAKOVA'S
SCHOOL OF BALLET

# Darcey's Magical Masterclass

## The Doll's Pirouette

*In Enchantia, dolls can come to life!*
*Dance to a waltz like the beautiful doll Coppelia,*
*with this pretty pirouette movement.*

**1.**
Start with your right
foot behind your left
foot and bend your
knees. Hold your
arms in front of you
(this is 4th position
with arms as well).

**2.**

Rise up on to the tiptoe of your left foot and pull your right foot up to your knee in one movement, using your right foot to push yourself into a turn. Swish your right arm out to the side.

**3.**

Bring your arms back together in front of you and lower your right foot, bending your knees back into a *demi-plié*. Your beautiful pirouette is complete!

### Magic Ballerina
#### Summer in Enchantia

A band of pirates has stolen the King and Queen's treasure! Can Rosa get it back before the summer party is ruined?

**Read on for a sneak preview of *Summer in Enchantia*...**

Rosa spun round and round and then the magic gently set her down. As the cloud of colours faded, her feet met something soft and grainy under her feet. *Sand!* Hearing the cry of seagulls in the air, she looked about. She was standing on a sunny beach with trees behind her and a blue sea lapping at the shore. There was a sharp tang of salt and seaweed in the air and far out on the water was a large old-fashioned ship with three masts and rectangular sails.

*I wonder why the shoes have brought me here?* she thought excitedly.

The sound of music and shouting drifted across the waves from the ship. The sailors on board seemed to be having a party. A black flag with a white picture was flying from the mast. Rosa looked closer and caught her breath. It was the skull and crossbones. That must mean it was a pirate ship!

Rosa wasn't too sure if she wanted to meet pirates. She started to back away uncertainly towards the trees when she heard a voice.

"Rosa! Over here!"

Rosa recognised it instantly. "Nutmeg!" she called, looking round. "Where are you?"

Nutmeg poked her head out from round one of the trees. "Over here!"

"So what's going on?" Rosa asked.

"We've got a big problem," said Nutmeg. "And it's all to do with those pirates…"

# Darcey Bussell

Buy more great Magic Ballerina books direct from HarperCollins at 10% off recommended retail price.
FREE postage and packing in the UK.

All priced at £3.99

To purchase by Visa/Mastercard/Switch simply call
**08707871724** or fax on **08707871725**

To pay by cheque, send a copy of this form with a cheque made payable to
'HarperCollins Publishers' to: Mail Order Dept. (Ref: BOB4),
HarperCollins Publishers, Westerhill Road, Bishopbriggs, G64 2QT,
making sure to include your full name, postal address and phone number.

From time to time HarperCollins may wish to use your personal data
to send you details of other HarperCollins publications and offers.
If you wish to receive information on other HarperCollins publications
and offers please tick this box ☐